All quotes included in this book are from the shooting script and may not appear in the final cut of the movie.

First published 2013 by Walker Books Ltd
87 Vauxhall Walk, London SE11 5HJ

10 9 8 7 6 5 4 3 2 1

Printed and bound in China

British Library Cataloguing in Publication Data:
a catalogue record for this book is available from the British Library

ISBN 978-1-4063-5199-6
www.walker.co.uk

THE
MORTAL INSTRUMENTS
City of Bones

THE LITTLE
BOOK of
QUOTES

WALKER
BOOKS

"Welcome to the City of Bones."

Jace

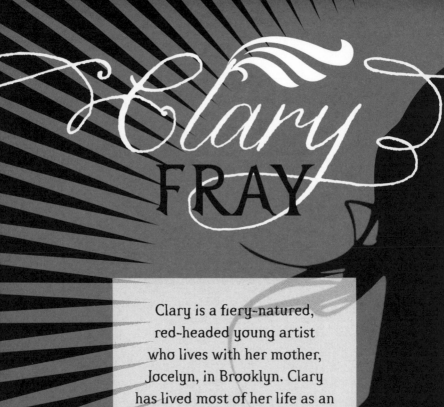

Clary
FRAY

Clary is a fiery-natured,
red-headed young artist
who lives with her mother,
Jocelyn, in Brooklyn. Clary
has lived most of her life as an
ordinary girl, unaware of her
family's past or her mother's
Shadowhunter nature. Until
she meets Jace Wayland.

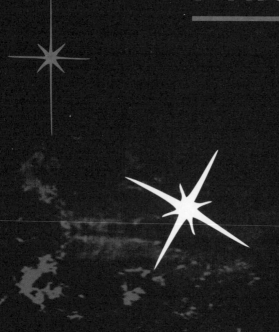

I PASSED OUT
AND YOU GUYS TAT

I THOUGHT

TOO ME?

THAT ONLY

happened

IN

VEGAS

YOU MIGHT NOT
KNOW MUCH ABOUT
*mundane
history*

BUT
I CAN
TELL
YOU

WHEN PEOPLE START
TALKING ABOUT
PRESERVING RACE
AND CLEANSING
BLOODLINES

IT
NEVER
GOES
WELL

WHEN GIRLS SAY

THEY WANT A BIG ROCK

THEY DON'T MEAN
LITERALLY A BIG ROCK

CLARY: GO AHEAD, HANG YOUR HEAD OUT THE WINDOW IF YOU NEED TO.

LUKE:

I'M A Werewolf

NOT A Golden retriever

AFTER WHAT WE'VE BEEN THROUGH, I CAN'T LOSE YOU.

DON'T EVER
IMAGINE YOU AREN'T

IMPORTANT

TO ME.

DON'T EVEN SAY THAT,
OKAY?

CLARY:

Is this the part where you START TEARING OFF strips of YOUR SHIRT to bind my wounds?

JACE:

If you wanted me
to rip my clothes off,
YOU
SHOULD'VE
JUST ASKED.

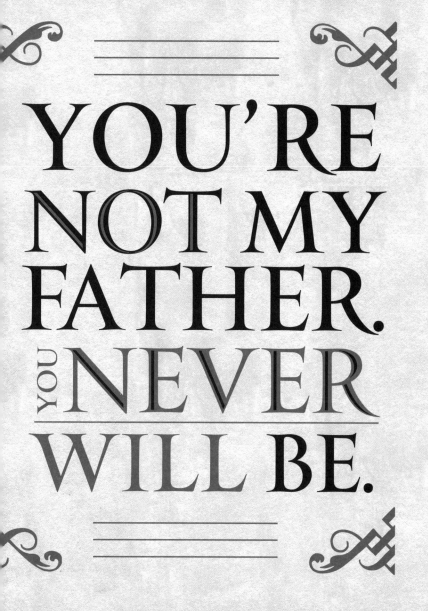

Bach
IS TO DEMONS
WHAT
garlic
IS TO VAMPIRES

Angelic Power

·THE MORTAL CUP·

JACE

HUNTER

WAYLAND

Since the death of his father
when he was ten, Jace –
young, handsome, and the
best Shadowhunter of his
generation – has lived in the
Institute with his adoptive
family, the Lightwoods. He has
a strong moral code despite his
tendency to break rules and
seek adventure.

UNFORTUNATELY *my* ON

tru

lo

Eve

REMAINS MYSELF

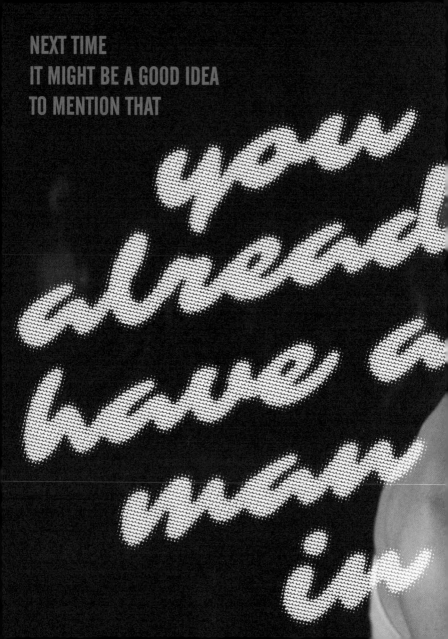

NEXT TIME
IT MIGHT BE A GOOD IDEA
TO MENTION THAT

you already have a man in

CLARY:

I KISSED YOU?

JACE:

DON'T WORRY
IT WASN'T
THAT

SPECIAL

FOR ME EITHER.

Don't tell me
■ You have a drawing ▶

EMERGENCY

You need a

nude model

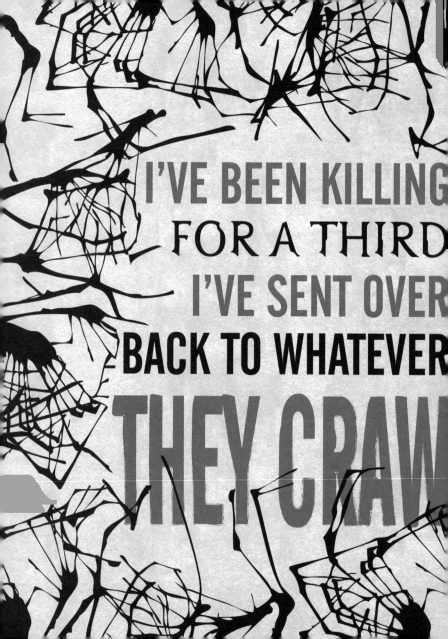

I'VE BEEN KILLING

FOR A THIRD

I'VE SENT OVER

BACK TO WHATEVER

THEY CRAW

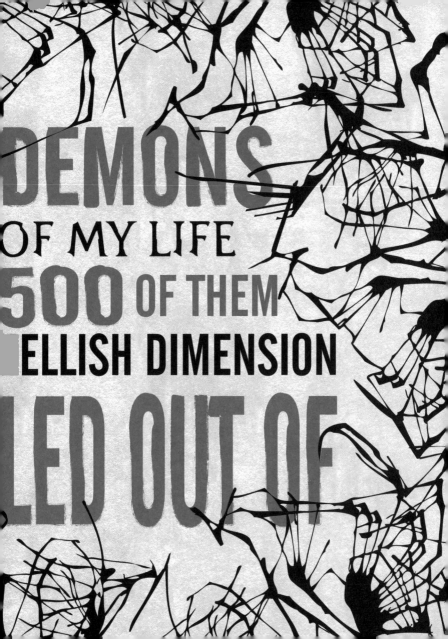

You're STILL THE BRAVEST MUNDANE I'VE EVER MET

I'D RATHER DIE WITH THEM

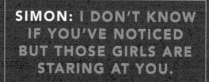

SIMON: I DON'T KNOW
IF YOU'VE NOTICED
BUT THOSE GIRLS ARE
STARING AT YOU.

JACE:

OF COURSE THEY ARE

I'M *stunningly* **ATTRACTIVE**

Love

THE WORLD HAS NOT CHANGED. YOU HAVE CHANGED.

SIMON LEWIS

Simon has been the best friend of Clary Fray since first grade. While as a mundane he may not be physically equipped to protect Clary from enemies, his courage and devotion to their friendship leads him into unusual situations.

I'd like
to report
a <u>public</u>
<u>nuisance.</u>

Well, he's a nuisance in <u>private</u>, too.

THANK GOD
THE
WEREWOLVES
~ ARE HERE TO ~
save us

*

I NEVER
THOUGHT
I'D SAY
THAT

IT'S MY FIRST TIME WITH THE

THROWER

YOU SHOULD SEE
ME AT SUDOKU

I GUESS
I'M A
ROMANTIC

I ALWAYS HOPED THAT WHEN I FINALLY SAID

"LOVE YOU"

to someone

SHE WOULD SAY THE SAME THING BACK

Did you DRINK *anything?*

YOU KNOW THOSE

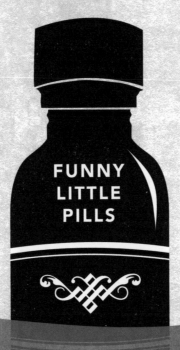

FUNNY
LITTLE
PILLS

AREN'T
CANDY

HALF
OF
Your
ATTENTION
IS BETTER THAN

ALL
OF ANYONE ELSE'S

Heightened
Speed

SHADOWHUNTERS

DOWNWORLDERS

Isabelle LIGHTWOOD

A Shadowhunter by trade and pedigree, Isabelle has a passion for sharp weapons, runes and all other accoutrements of demon hunting. Alec, Jace and Isabelle make a lethal team. While somewhat of an elitist when it comes to humans, at heart Isabelle is caring and loyal.

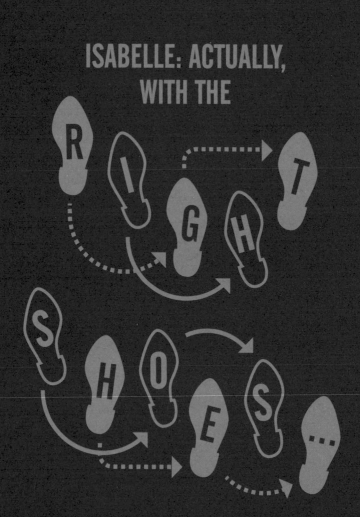

Clary: No, I mean,
I can't pull this off.

I'm **STUCK** *in this dress.*

*It's time you started
using some of*

your natur

feminine

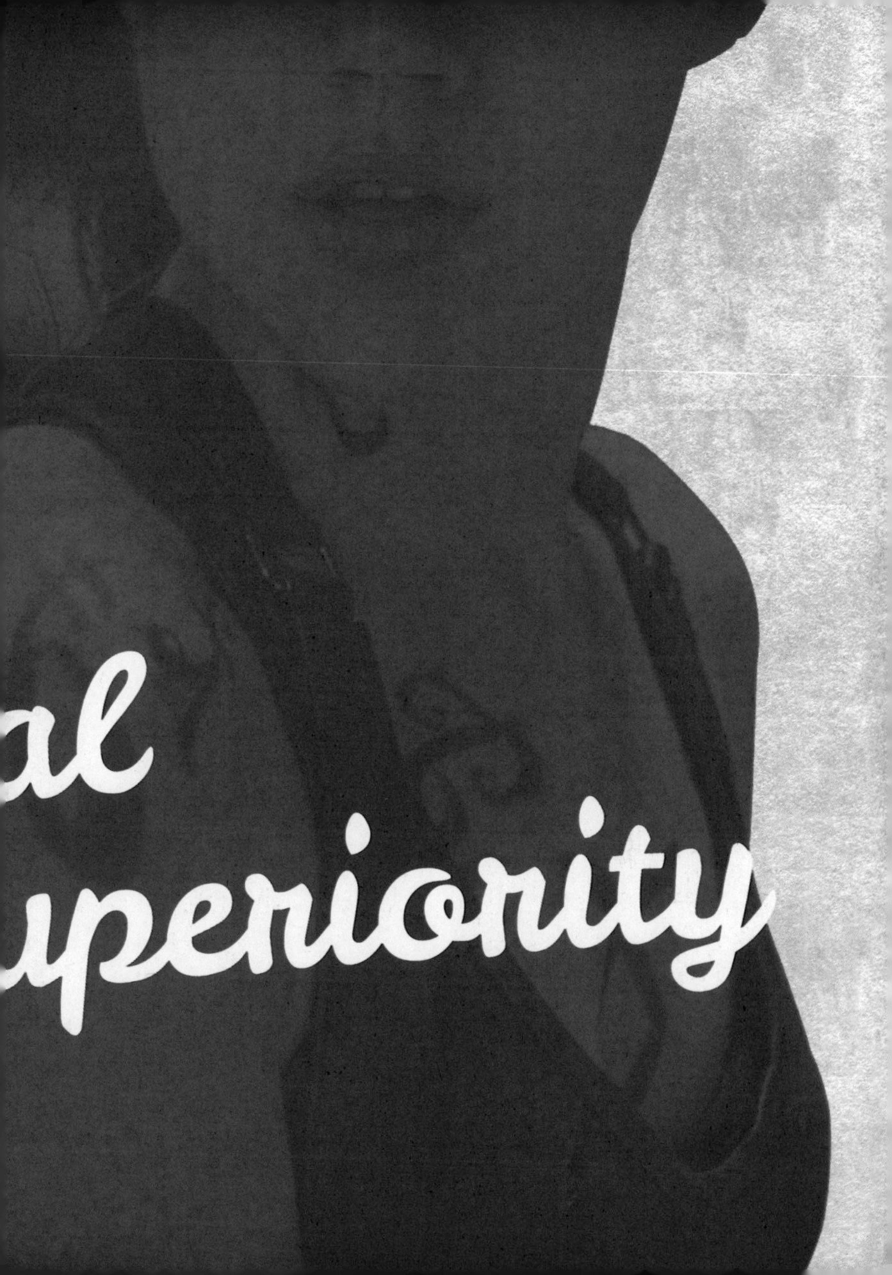
al
periority

SIMON: SO HOW DO YOU KILL A ZOMBIE?

ISABELLE: WE DON'T.

SIMON: OF COURSE. THEY'RE ALREADY DEAD.

ISABELLE: NO. THEY DON'T EXIST.

SIMON:

HOW MANY

DEMONS

ARE THERE?

∞

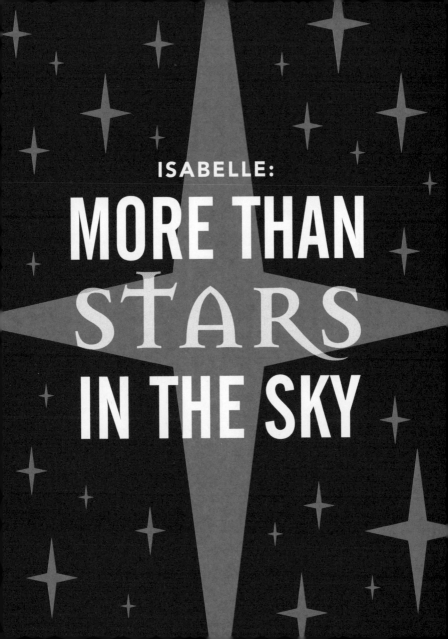

Stamina

_____

_____

_____

_____

_____

_____

_____

_____

_____

_____

ALEC

LIGHTWOOD

Alec is Isabelle's older brother and a resident of the New York Institute. However, any similarity Alec and Isabelle share in appearance, they lack in personality. Alec is very serious and uncomfortable around outsiders, while Isabelle is more of an extrovert.

YOU SLOW US DOWN

US DOWN

YOU'RE A
DEAD WEIGHT

A MUNDANE

WHAT IS IT ABOUT HER?

SHE'S BRAVE

WE'RE

SHADOWHUNTERS

• **WE'RE ALL** •

brave

JACE THINKS
HE NEEDS
TO SAVE
THE WORLD.

SOMETIMES I THINK
HE WANTS
TO DIE
TRYING.

Deflect / Block

_____

_____

_____

_____

_____

_____

_____

_____

_____

_____

MAGNUS BANE

Magnus Bane is the flamboyant High Warlock of Brooklyn. He enjoys entertaining and is well known for the lavish parties he throws exclusively for Downworlders at his loft. Magnus has lived for hundreds of years and despite his party-boy lifestyle, he's wise and unbelievably powerful.

EVERYONE THINKS IT'S SO GREAT
To Live forever
IT'S NOT

YOU BURY EVERYONE

you Love

NOTHING MUCH
IMPRESSES YOU
ANY MORE

There's a treasure map
inside your head, Clary.

Follow it

and it

will take
you

to
the TRUTH

Clairvoyant
Sight

_____

_____

_____

_____

_____

_____

_____

_____

_____

_____

VALENTINE
MORGENSTERN

Valentine is a powerful
Shadowhunter. Brilliant and
handsome, he was once the
leader of an exclusive group of
warriors known as the Circle.
Due to his radical agenda,
Valentine is a common
enemy of Downworlders and
Shadowhunters alike.

THE WORLD
IS OURS

TO TAKE

THERE'S NO TIME

TO
WASTE

WE HAVE FOUGHT THE DARKNESS SO LONG

We have FALLEN IN *Love* WITH THE SHADOWS

Equilibrium

_____

_____

_____

_____

_____

_____

_____

_____

_____

_____

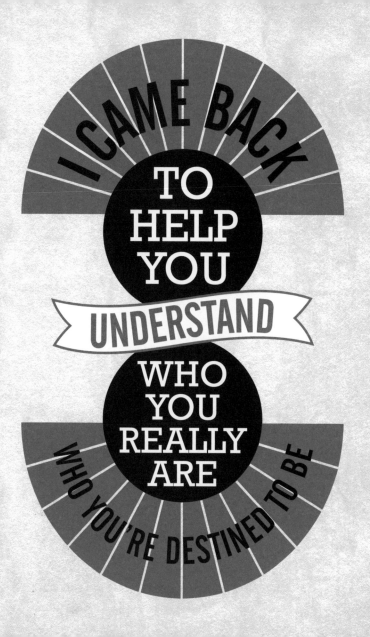